THE OPPOSITE ZOO

Il Sung Na

ALFRED A. KNOPF
NEW YORK

The sky is DARK, and the
Opposite Zoo is CLOSED.

But the monkey's door is OPEN!
Time to explore. . . .

AWAKE!

asleep . . .

Hairy

Bald

Tall

short

shy

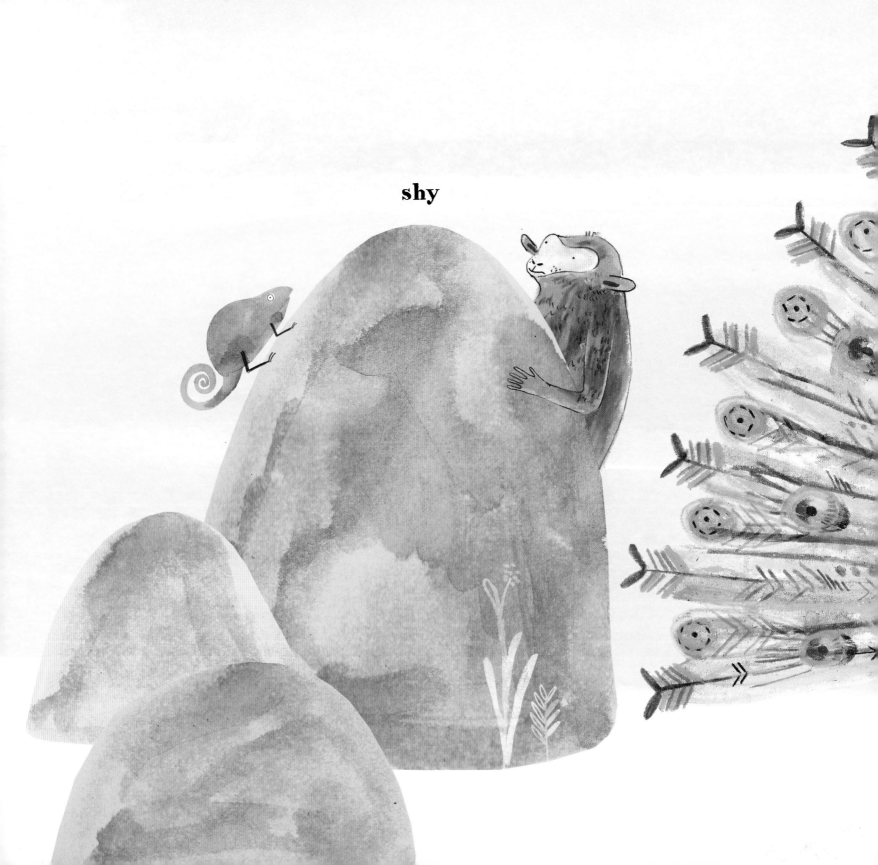

BOLD

Soft

prickly

Black

White

Slow

Fast

quiet

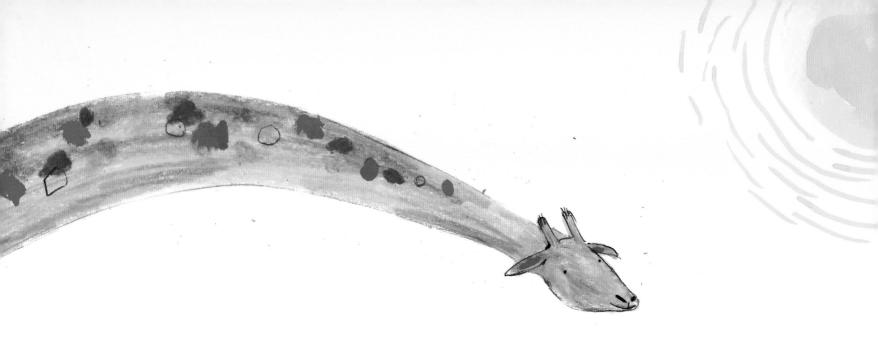

The sun is **BRIGHT**, and the animals are ready!

**The monkey's door CLOSES
just in time . . .**

THE OPPOSITE
ZOO

. . . for the Opposite
Zoo to OPEN!

To all who inspired me
to try opposites

THIS IS A BORZOI BOOK PUBLISHED BY ALFRED A. KNOPF

Copyright © 2016 by Il Sung Na

All rights reserved. Published in the United States by Alfred A. Knopf,
an imprint of Random House Children's Books,
a division of Penguin Random House LLC, New York.

Knopf, Borzoi Books, and the colophon
are registered trademarks of Penguin Random House LLC.

Visit us on the Web! randomhousekids.com

Educators and librarians, for a variety of teaching tools, visit us at RHTeachersLibrarians.com

Library of Congress Cataloging-in-Publication Data
Na, Il Sung, author, illustrator.
The opposite zoo / Il Sung Na. — First edition.
pages   cm.
Summary: After the zoo closes, monkey slips out of his cage to explore the
zoo, introducing the reader to the other animals and the idea of opposites.
ISBN 978-0-553-51127-7 (trade) — ISBN 978-0-553-51128-4 (lib. bdg.) —
ISBN 978-0-553-51129-1 (ebook)
1. Monkeys—Juvenile fiction. 2. Zoos—Juvenile fiction. 3. Animals—Juvenile
fiction. 4. Polarity—Juvenile fiction. [1. Monkeys—Fiction. 2. Zoos—Fiction. 3. Zoo
animals—Fiction. 4. English language—Antonyms and synonyms—Fiction.] I. Title.
PZ7.N1244Op 2016
[E]—dc23
2014043816

Also available as an ebook

MANUFACTURED IN CHINA

March 2016

10 9 8 7 6 5 4 3 2 1

First Edition